Mommy Is a Soft, Warm Kiss

Rhonda Gowler Greene

illustrated by Maggie Smith

Walker & Company
New York

First published in the United States of America in April 2010 by
Walker Publishing Company, Inc., a division of Bloomsbury Publishing, Inc.
Visit Walker & Company's Web site at www.bloomsburykids.com

For information about permission to reproduce selections from this book, write to
Permissions, Walker & Company, 175 Fifth Avenue, New York, New York 10010

Library of Congress Cataloging-in-Publication Data
Greene, Rhonda Gowler.
Mommy is a soft, warm kiss / Rhonda Gowler Greene ; illustrated by Maggie Smith.
p.   cm.
Summary: A child celebrates all of the wonderful things a mother can be throughout the year,
from a treasure buried in summer sand to a snow-white angel gliding down winter slopes.
ISBN-13: 978-0-8027-9729-2 · ISBN-10: 0-8027-9729-6
[1. Stories in rhyme. 2. Mother and child—Fiction. 3. Seasons—Fiction. 4. Year—Fiction.] I. Smith, Maggie, ill. II. Title.
PZ8.3.G824Mom 2010   [E]—dc22   2008013355

Book design by Nicole Gastonguay
Typeset in Sassoon Sans
Art created with watercolors and acrylics on 140-lb cold-pressed paper

Printed in China by L. Rex Printing Co. Ltd., Dongguan, Guangdong
2 4 6 8 10 9 7 5 3 1

All papers used by Walker & Company are natural, recyclable products
made from wood grown in well-managed forests. The manufacturing processes
conform to the environmental regulations of the country of origin.

For my sweet mom,

and for Matt, who said I was his rocking chair

—R. G. G.

For Audrey and her mommy, Cynthia

—M. S.

Mommy is the sprinkle rain for seeds all in a row.
She helps me plant a garden.
We wait for it to grOW.

Mommy is a ticklebug that
makes me squirm and giggle.
Her fingers creep-crawl
in and out . . .

and make me laugh and wiggle.

Mommy is a buried treasure
in the sand and sun.
I cover her . . . discover her!

Seashell Stories

What silly summer fun!

Mommy is a caterpillar
in her snug cocoon.
I cuddle up beside her
beneath a circle moon.

Mommy is a rocking chair
when time to take a nap.
Back and forth I rock and doze,
cozy in her lap.

Mommy is a thread that's dancing, bobbing up and down,

sewing purple polka dots—

so I can be a clown!

Mommy is a yummy smell
of pumpkin pie, so sweet.
We share a meal with company,
give thanks,
then eat
and eat!

Mommy is an angel,
with snow-white, whisper wings,
who glides with me down slippery slopes
and laughs and plays and sings.

Mommy is my noodle soup when I am sick in bed.
She stays with me and reads me books
and cools my achy head.

Mommy is a happy tune I keep inside my heart—
a tune she taught that we both hum
when we are far apart.

Mommy is a yellow duck that loves a rainy day.

We splash and splat together
and *quack!* and plip-plop play.

Mommy is a soft, warm kiss when tucking me in tight.

We make a wish upon a star,
then whisper, "Nighty-night."

Mommy is so many things with me

the whole year through.

I'm glad I have my mommy . . .

Mommy,
I love you.